The Case of the Soccer Camp Mystery

Book created by Parker C. Hinter

Written by Della Rowland

Illustrated by Diamond Studio

Based on characters from the Parker Brothers game

A Creative Media Applications Production

SCHOLASTIC INC.
New York Toronto London Auckland Sydney

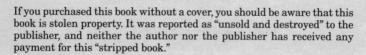

ISBN 0-590-13788-3

12 11 10 9 8 7 6 5 4 3 2 1   8 9/9 0 1 2 3/0

Printed in the U.S.A.   40

First Scholastic printing, April 1998

Contents

The Case of the Mixed-up Students

It was Parents' Night at the elementary school, the night parents go to school instead of their children. That day at school, the Clue Jr. Club kids were waiting for the first bell to ring and talking to Danny Dot, a new kid in school.

"So what happens on Parents' Night?" Danny asked the kids.

"Your parents go to all your classes," began Mortimer.

"You make a list of your classes and leave it on your desk for them," explained Samantha. "Then they spend ten minutes in each one of your classes. That way they get to see what you're studying."

"We did something like that at my old school," said Danny.

"Did you have to clean out your desk, too?" asked Peter, making a face. Peter's desk and locker were always a mess.

Brrrrrriiiiiing! The bell rang and the kids all lined up at the entrance doors and filed into the school. During the period before lunch, Ms. Redding helped her fourth-grade students write out their class schedules. "Don't forget to leave your list on top of your desk when you leave today," she reminded them.

Danny Dot raised his hand with a question just as the lunch bell rang. "Ask Rusty to help you, Danny," Ms. Redding told him. She pointed to Rusty Red, who sat next to Danny. "I'm on lunch duty today and have to leave right now. If you have any more questions, I'll answer them after lunch."

"Okay," said Danny, taking his list of classes to Rusty's desk.

Mortimer brought his list to the lunchroom to show the others. He asked Greta to read it out loud.

"First period: social studies. Second

period: health or gym. Third period: math. Fourth period: English. Fifth period: LUNCH!" Greta started giggling. "Mortimer, you wrote *lunch* in huge letters."

"Go on," he said.

Greta continued reading. "Sixth period: reading. Seventh period: art or music. Eighth period." She stopped reading and looked up. "Eighth period?" she said. "We don't have an eighth period."

"Yes, we do," chuckled Mortimer. "Keep reading."

"Eighth period," Greta said. "Pizza."

"Eighth period," Mortimer said. "That's when we go to the pizza parlor after school!" Everyone burst into laughter.

After lunch, Ms. Redding handed out test papers. Rusty Red didn't answer when his name was called. "Does anyone know where Rusty is?" she asked.

"He didn't feel good at lunch, so he went to the nurse," Danny told her. "Maybe he went home."

That afternoon, Ms. Redding had the

children clean their desks and lockers. During art class, they drew pictures of their families and hung them around the room. By the last period, the classroom looked neat and cheerful. Finally, the dismissal bell rang. The Clue Jr. kids got their jackets from their lockers and started for the exit doors.

"Oh, wait," Greta told the others. "I forgot my math book." She ran back to Ms. Redding's class. As she hurried through the classroom door, she bumped into Ray Red, Rusty's older brother, who was coming out. "Oops, sorry," she said.

"That's okay," said Ray.

"Did Rusty go home sick?" asked Samantha.

"Yeah," said Ray. "I came to get his homework."

"Do you know which desk is his?" asked Peter.

"Yeah, his class schedule was on top of it," said Ray.

Greta came out of the classroom holding

4

up her math book. "I got my book," she said. "I'm ready to go to eighth period."

The kids headed off to the pizza parlor.

The next morning the fourth-grade class was noisy with kids talking about their parents' going to school last night.

"Class, I want you to put away the schedules for now," said Ms. Redding. "We'll talk about Parents' Night during our free period this afternoon."

"Awww," said the kids in unison. Disappointed, they stuck the schedules inside their desks.

"Here it is," said Danny Dot, pulling a pencil box from his desk.

"What?" asked Samantha, whose desk was in front of Danny's.

"My pencil box," whispered Danny, holding it up. "My folks said they couldn't find it last night when they were looking through my desk. My uncle sent it to me. He lives in Detroit."

Samantha looked at the pencil box. It was a blue car. "Cool," she said.

"Wait!" Danny said, looking into his desk. "Some of my books are gone."

Ms. Redding came over. "Is anything wrong, Danny?" she said.

"A couple of my books are gone," he said.

"Did your parents take them last night by mistake?" she asked.

"No," said Danny, shaking his head.

"Well, borrow Rusty's books today," she told Danny. "He's still absent. We'll try to get this sorted out after school."

Danny took some textbooks from Rusty's desk and went back to his desk.

After school, Ms. Redding called Danny up to her desk and asked the Clue Jr. kids to wait for him. She wrote down the books that were missing and told him to take the list to the lost and found. "Would you please show Danny where the lost and found office is?" she asked the kids.

"Sure," said Peter. "Come on, Danny."

"Wait," Samantha said. "I don't think Danny's books are lost."

"No?" said Ms. Redding.

"I think Rusty has them," said Samantha.

"But he went home sick yesterday," said Mortimer. "How could he have taken them?"

"He didn't," said Samantha. "But he has them."

"Now I'm really confused," said Ms. Redding.

"Yeah, Samantha," said Peter. "How can Rusty have Danny's books if he didn't take them?"

How does Samantha think Rusty got Danny's books?

SOLUTION:
The Case of the Mixed-up Students

"Because his brother Ray took them," said Samantha. "Yesterday, remember?"

"Yeah," said Mortimer. "But he took Rusty's books."

"That's what he *thought*," said Saman- tha. "He saw Rusty's list of classes on top of a desk, so he thought that desk was Rusty's."

"It wasn't?" said Ms. Redding.

"No," said Samantha. "Look on Rusty's desk. A class list is still on top because he's not here today."

Sure enough, Danny's list was on Rusty's desk. "We must have mixed them up when Rusty was helping me yesterday at lunchtime," said Danny.

"I see," said Greta. "When Ray came to get Rusty's homework, he saw the list with Rusty's name on Danny's desk."

"So he took the books from Danny's desk instead of Rusty's," finished Peter.

"Right," said Mortimer. "And last night, Danny's parents thought Rusty's desk was Danny's. That's why they couldn't find the pencil box inside."

"Whew!" Greta sighed. "I think we finally straightened out the big desk mix-up."

"Good," said Mortimer. "Then we'd better hurry or we'll be late for eighth period."

"Eighth period?" said Danny. "There isn't any eighth period."

The kids started laughing and headed for the pizza parlor.

10

The Case of the Missing Ice

One Sunday afternoon in early spring, Samantha Scarlet called the other members of the Clue Jr. Club. She was in a panic. "We've got a case," she said. "A very important one. Come over right away!"

When Peter Plum, Mortimer Mustard, and Greta Green arrived, Samantha took them up to her parents' bedroom. "My mom's diamond engagement ring is missing from her dresser," she told them. "Dad was looking for it this morning. He wants to have the ring cleaned for their anniversary."

Greta's eyes got wide. "There was a robbery in your house?" she asked.

"No," said Samantha. "This is worse. I think Petunia took the ring and hid it somewhere."

"Your parrot took your mom's ring?" Peter said.

"Why would she do that?" asked Mortimer.

"Petunia likes shiny things," Samantha answered. "She calls them *pretty-pretty*. Sometimes she picks them up. I've seen her look at that ring on Mom's finger. If I can't find the ring, Petunia will really be in trouble. And so will I."

"Maybe your mom is wearing her ring," said Peter.

"No," said Samantha, shaking her head. "She's on a business trip. She never wears that ring when she goes away because she doesn't want to lose it."

"When will your mom be back?" said Mortimer.

"At the end of the week," said Samantha. "If I can't find the ring, Mom will be really upset. She loves that ring. She calls it her ice."

"What's that mean?" asked Greta.

"Ice? It means diamond," answered Samantha.

"I have an idea," said Mortimer. "Let's look around your mom's dresser. Maybe it fell on the floor somewhere."

"Then let's check out the rest of the house," said Peter. "Maybe we'll find Petunia's hiding spot."

The kids helped Samantha look for the ring all afternoon, but it was nowhere to be found. Suddenly the grandfather clock in Samantha's living room chimed five times.

"Wow! It's five o'clock already," said Greta. "I have to go home for dinner."

"Me, too," Mortimer said.

"We'll come back after school tomorrow and look some more," Peter said.

"Don't worry, Samantha, we'll find the ring," Greta said.

"Okay, guys," Samantha said. "Thanks."

That night a late-season snowstorm dumped freezing snow on the town. School was closed on Monday, so the kids came to

Samantha's to play outside and look for the ring. They spent the morning making snow people and having snowball fights.

"Can you believe this snow?" said Greta. "It's supposed to be spring."

"I know," said Mortimer. "Yesterday it was almost hot."

"Hey! We have a day off from school," said Peter. "I'm not complaining."

After making snow angels in the backyard, the kids had hot cocoa and cookies upstairs in Samantha's room — all except Greta. She was still out in the backyard trying to make the perfect angel. Samantha took Petunia out of her cage. "You're a bad bird," she scolded. "I looked for Mom's ring again last night and I still couldn't find it," she told the others. "I'm really getting worried."

"Maybe a game of Clue Jr. would give us some ideas," said Mortimer.

"Good thinking," said Samantha. "Let's tell Greta to come up." She opened the window and yelled down to Greta. When she

did, Petunia flew out of the open window cawing, "Pretty-pretty."

"Petunia's getting out!" cried Peter.

Peter and Mortimer rushed to the window as Petunia flew down into the backyard.

"It's okay, Peter," Samantha told him. "She does this all the time." She stuck her head out the window and called down to Greta, "Petunia must like the shiny sparkles on your hat, Greta!"

"Won't Petunia get cold outside?" asked Mortimer.

"Don't worry, she'll come right back in," said Samantha. "She likes to splash in the birdbath. When she realizes the water in it is frozen, she'll come back."

Greta came up and the kids began playing a game of Clue Jr. After a while, Peter decided he had the mystery solved. "I think the bird is in the mailbox," he announced.

"Speaking of birds, did Petunia come back inside?" asked Mortimer.

"Oh, yeah," said Samantha. "A long time ago. I told you she wouldn't stay out very long. She can't take a bath in ice!"

"Wait! I've got it!" exclaimed Mortimer.

"What? Peter already solved this Clue Jr. case," said Greta.

"No, not the game," Mortimer said. "The ice! I know where your mom's ice is."

"Great, Mortimer!" exclaimed Samantha. "Where is it?"

"On ice," answered Mortimer.

Where does Mortimer think the missing ring is?

17

"No," said Samantha. "She went to the birdbath and started pecking at it."

The kids dashed to the birdbath and peered into it. Sure enough, there was Mrs. Scarlet's engagement ring, frozen in the ice.

"How did it get here?" asked Greta.

"We had the windows open earlier this week when it was warm," said Samantha. "Petunia must have picked up the ring. Then she flew outside to take a bath and dropped the ring in the birdbath."

"Good job, Mortimer," said Peter. "You solved this case."

"Now let's see if Petunia can solve a game of Clue Jr.," laughed Mortimer.

SOLUTION:
The Case of the Missing Ice

"It's in the backyard," said Mortimer. The kids threw on their coats and ran out-side.

"Hurry and tell us, Mortimer," said Samantha, looking around. "It's freezing out here."

"When you said Petunia couldn't take a bath in ice, I remembered something," Mortimer told Samantha. "What was she saying when she flew out the window?"

"She was saying, *pretty-pretty*," said Greta.

"That's right," said Peter. "Samantha said that's what she says when she sees something shiny."

"Yeah, she saw Greta's sparkly hat," Samantha said.

"Maybe," said Mortimer. "But what did she do? She didn't fly over to Greta."

The Case of the
One-of-a-kind Kite

It was a windy day — perfect weather to fly a kite. The Clue Jr. Club decided to pack lunches and bike over to Flannel Field with their kites. Before they even got to the field, they could see a few kites in the air.

"Look," said Greta, pointing to the sky. "Some other kids are already there."

"Look at all of the different patterns on the kites," said Mortimer.

A few minutes later, the kids pedaled into Flannel Field. They laid their bikes on the ground with several others.

"Let's find some clear sky and get our kites up there, too!" exclaimed Greta. They grabbed their kites and ran for an open space in the field.

"Look at that one," said Mortimer while

they were getting their kites ready. He pointed up to a black-and-yellow kite with an unusual dragon design.

"Wow!" exclaimed Peter. "What a cool design!"

"I've never seen anything like that," said Greta. "It's beautiful."

Soon all of the Clue Jr. kids had their kites flying in the air. For an hour, they ran back and forth pulling their kites behind them.

"I think it's time for lunch," said Mortimer. "I'm going to pull my kite in."

"I'm hungry," Peter agreed.

"Me, too," said Greta.

"Me, three," said Samantha.

The kids brought their kites down. Then they headed back to their bikes, where they had their lunch bags.

"Hey!" Samantha exclaimed when they reached their bikes. "What's this?"

"Our tires!" said Greta. "They're all flat."

Mortimer frowned. "What a drag!"

"And I didn't bring my pump today," said Peter. "I didn't want to carry it *and* my kite."

"Great," said Samantha. "We'll have to push our bikes all the way home."

"It's too far to do that," said Greta. "We'll have to call one of our parents to come get us."

"The nearest phone is all the way in the parking lot," said Mortimer. "Well, I say we eat before we do anything."

The kids ate their lunch, then began walking their bikes to the field's parking lot. When they reached the phone, several other kids with bikes were in line to use the phone.

"Look! Their tires are flat, too," said Samantha.

"What happened?" Peter asked one of them.

"We were playing tennis on the courts over there," the kid explained. "When we came back to get our bikes, someone had let the air out of our tires."

Peter's jaw dropped. "Wow!" he exclaimed. "Someone's going to be in big trouble."

"If they get caught," said one of the kids. "Which they probably won't."

Just then Officer Lawford came walking across the parking lot with an angry man. They walked over to another group of boys who were holding kites. "That's one of them, Officer Lawford," the man said. He pointed to one of the boys.

"One of what?" said the boy rudely.

"What's your name, son?" Officer Lawford asked the boy.

"Ronnie Rhubarb," the boy replied.

"Well, Ronnie, this gentleman says he saw you letting the air out of a bicycle tire," Officer Lawford said.

"It wasn't me," said Ronnie. "I've been over in Flannel Field flying my kite." He held up his kite to show Officer Lawford.

"That's a remarkable kite," said Officer Lawford. "That dragon is very unusual."

"Yep," said Ronnie. "It's one of a kind."

"Well, I see some other kids here with kites," said Officer Lawford. "Let's see if any of them saw your kite today." He motioned for the Clue Jr. Club kids to come over.

"Were you kids flying kites in Flannel Field today?" he asked them.

"Yes, sir," Peter answered.

"Did you see this kite in the sky?" Officer Lawford asked.

"Yeah!" said Mortimer. "We noticed it right away. None of us had ever seen a kite like it before."

"Of course." Ronnie smirked. "Like I said, it's one of a kind."

"Right," said Greta. "And that's why we know *you* weren't flying it this morning."

"What are you talking about?" yelled Ronnie. "All your friends just said they saw it."

"I saw it, too," said Greta.

"What are you getting at, young lady?" asked Officer Lawford.

"I think he's the one who's been letting air out of tires," answered Greta.

Why does Greta think Ronnie wasn't flying the kite?

SOLUTION:
The Case of the One-of-a-kind Kite

"Why do you think that?" asked Officer Lawford.

"Because Ronnie wasn't flying the kite," answered Greta.

"Do you know who was?" asked Officer Lawford.

"No, but I know it was a she, not a he," said Greta.

"Oh, yeah," said Mortimer. "There was a *girl* flying that kite. I noticed that right when we came into the park."

"Which means it couldn't be Ronnie," said Peter.

"They're right," Ronnie confessed. "It was my sister flying the kite. I have it because I was going to fly it after lunch."

"And I guess your friends here were helping you with the tires?" asked Officer Lawford. Caught, Ronnie nodded.

"Now you and your pals can fill all these

bicycle tires back up," said Officer Lawford, handing Ronnie a tire pump.

"You'll be like the wind today," Peter
told Ronnie. "Only you won't be flying any
kites."

The Case of the
Messed-up Cleanup

The days were getting warmer and, best of all, spring break from school was coming up. Peter's father, Mr. Plum, decided this would be a good time to clean out the basement. "How about you kids helping me?" he asked the Clue Jr. Club. "I'll treat you all to pizza and a movie as a reward."

Peter, Samantha, Mortimer, and Greta thought this was a great idea. On the first day of their spring vacation, they arrived at Peter's house bright and early.

"Come on in. Peter is in the backyard playing with Bosco," Mrs. Plum told the kids when she answered the door. She handed Greta a plastic trash bag. "Can you give Peter this to put in the trash can?" Mrs. Plum asked.

"Hi, guys," Peter called out as the kids

walked around to the backyard. He was petting his dog, Bosco. "You're just in time to help me."

"What's up?" asked Mortimer.

"I got Bosco a new plastic bone," Peter explained. "The old one is his favorite toy, but there's almost nothing left of it." He pointed to a shredded bone. "I'm going to throw him the new bone. When he chases it, grab the old one and put it in the trash."

"Gotcha," Greta said.

"Fetch, boy!" Peter threw the toy bone and Bosco dashed after it.

Greta quickly picked up the old bone with two fingers. "Yuck," she said. "This thing is gross."

"Let me see," Mortimer said. He peered at the shredded toy and made a face. "That bone looks pretty gross," he said. Bosco came bounding back and tried to get his old toy from Greta.

"Here, Greta!" said Peter. "Put it in the trash can." Greta dropped the toy into the can. Then Peter quickly put the lid on. He picked up the new bone and threw it again. Bosco leaped up and caught the toy in midair. Then he padded over to his doghouse, flopped down, and began to chew on it happily.

"There!" Peter exclaimed. "I knew he'd go for it. Come on. I'll show you what we're supposed to do today."

Peter took his friends to the basement and showed them what to clean. Mr. Plum had already made piles of junk to be thrown out. There were also several recycling bins filled with plastic bottles, glass bottles, and cans.

"Dad wants us to put all this trash into plastic bags and carry it outside," Peter told everyone. "He also wants us to pull down the cobwebs, then sweep the floor and mop it."

"Where do we start?" asked Greta.

"First let's take out these recycling bins," Peter said. "Dad can take them to the recycling center when he gets home from work." Everyone grabbed a bin and hauled it up the basement stairs into the backyard. The trash can next to the shed was on its side, so Peter picked it up and put the lid back on. Then the kids arranged the recycling bins neatly beside it.

While they were outside, Bob Beet, a fourth-grader who lived in the neighborhood, came by and asked the kids what they were doing. When he heard the reward was pizza and a free movie, he wanted to help clean, too.

"That's okay," said Peter. "There're four of us. We don't really need any more help."

"You wouldn't really help anyway," Mortimer told him. "You just want to go to the movies."

"Right, like the way you helped me and Mortimer on the science project," said Greta. "You sat around and let everybody else do all the work. Then you got angry because we didn't want to put your name on it."

"I did not!" Bob exclaimed angrily. "Forget it! I was just trying to help." He stormed off down the street.

After Bob left, the kids went down to the basement to start filling trash bags. When they brought the bags up the stairs, they found the trash can overturned again, so Peter picked it up. Each time they came up from the basement with another trash bag, the can was turned over.

"I know it's Bob," muttered Greta. "He's trying to get even with us for not letting him help."

Finally the cleaning was finished and the kids headed off to the movies. When they returned, Mrs. Plum told them Mr. Plum wanted to see them right away. Mr. Plum was in the backyard and he was mad. "Look at this," he said, pointing to the yard. The trash can was overturned. Trash bags were ripped open and there was trash scattered all over the ground.

"It must be Bob Beet," Peter told his dad. "He wanted to help so he could go to

the movies for free. When we said no, he got mad. He must be messing with the trash cans to get even."

"When we went to the movies, I bet he ripped open all the bags and threw garbage all over the yard," said Greta.

"Wait," said Samantha. "It wasn't Bob."

"Who, then?" asked Mr. Plum.

"I see five clues," Samantha said. "Four are standing in front of us. The fifth one is in the trash."

What evidence does Samantha see? Who turned over the trash can?

boy!" Peter picked up the shredded plastic bone and threw it across the yard. Every-one laughed as Bosco ran after it happily.

"Everyone knows dogs love leftovers," Mortimer said.

SOLUTION:
The Case of the Messed-up Cleanup

Samantha pointed to the recycling bins. "There are the first four clues," she said. "The recycling bins haven't been touched."

"What does that mean?" asked Mr. Plum.

"Well," Samantha said, "if Bob wanted to make a mess, he would have turned over the recycling bins, too."

"Yeah, whoever did this only turned over the trash can," said Peter.

"Wait! The can was turned over *before* Bob even came over," said Greta.

"Right," said Samantha. Then she pointed inside the can. "There's the fifth clue."

"Bosco's old bone?" said Peter.

"I get it!" exclaimed Mortimer. "Bosco was trying to get his old toy bone."

"That's right," said Samantha. "He still wants it!"

"Okay, Bosco," said Peter. "Here you go,"

5

The Case of the Stolen Cookies

It was Monday morning, the first day after spring break. Peter arrived at school wearing a new T-shirt he got on a family trip to Sea City Marina. It was white with a huge blue-and-green shark on the front.

On the playground, all the kids were talking about what they did during their break. Everyone was having a hard time adjusting to being at school again after a week's vacation. However, they all perked up when Mortimer reminded them what day it was.

"Hey, this is a great day to come back to school," said Mortimer.

"Why?" exclaimed Greta.

"Because it's pizza day," he reminded them. "Remember? Every Monday and

Thursday this month, the eighth grade is having a pizza and cookie sale at lunch."

"Oh, yeah," said Samantha. "They're trying to raise money for their class trip."

"I just hope they have enough pizza," Mortimer worried. "I need more than one slice."

At lunchtime, the Clue Jr. Club kids raced to the cafeteria to line up for pizza. Mortimer hurried over to the cookie table to see what kind of cookies were being sold. When he got back in line he exclaimed, "It's chocolate chip! My favorite."

"A perfect lunch." Greta smiled. "Pizza and chocolate chip cookies!"

The kids got their pizza and cookies and found a table. While they were eating, Peter dribbled tomato sauce on his new T-shirt. "Oh, no!" he said. "My brand-new shirt is ruined."

"No, it isn't," said Samantha. "My mom told me how to get pizza sauce off. You

have to put soap and really cold water on the stain right away."

"Quick!" said Greta. "Go to the bathroom and wash it off."

"Okay, I'll try," said Peter. He hurried out of the cafeteria to the bathroom.

In a few minutes, Peter came back holding a big wet spot on his shirt away from his chest. Mortimer started laughing. "The pizza sauce was only a dot," he said to Peter. "It looks like you washed your whole shirt."

As Peter sat down, the lunch monitor walked over to him.

"Is everything all right, Peter?" she asked. "Where did you disappear to?"

"I went to the bathroom," he answered.

"Did you forget that you're supposed to have permission to leave the cafeteria?" she asked.

"Oops," Peter said. "I had to wash out my T-shirt quickly. I got pizza sauce on it."

"Well, you're right. You have to wash out a tomato sauce stain immediately," said the lunch monitor. "But it only takes a second to ask permission, so make sure you don't leave again without permission. Okay?"

"Sure," said Peter. "Sorry."

"Let's see your shirt," said Samantha, peering at the wet spot. "It looks pretty good, Peter."

"Yeah," said Greta. "I bet after it gets washed in the machine, it'll look fine."

"Good." Peter sighed. "My parents would kill me if I ruined this T-shirt the very first time I wore it."

After the kids finished eating, Mortimer decided he wanted another cookie.

"I hope they still have some," Peter said.

The four friends walked up to the cookie table. Eleanor and Barry, two eighth-graders, were selling the cookies. They said there weren't any more left.

"There were a lot left when I went to get more napkins," said Barry. "But they were almost all gone when I came back."

"A lot of kids bought them," said Eleanor.

"Everyone loves chocolate chip cookies," said Greta.

"We've never sold all of the cookies at a sale before," said Barry. "This is great. I bet we made a lot of money today." He got out a piece of paper and a pencil and started writing down some figures.

"What are you doing?" asked Eleanor.

"I'm figuring out how much money we made," Barry answered. "There were twenty cookies in each box, and we had eight boxes. That makes one hundred sixty cookies. Each cookie cost fifty cents." Barry did some quick multiplication. "That comes to eighty dollars," he said. "Come on, Eleanor, let's take our money to the office."

"Next time you have chocolate chip cookies, bring ten boxes!" Peter laughed.

The next morning, the Clue Jr. kids were standing on the playground waiting for the bell to ring. Mr. Higgins, the principal, walked over to them with Eleanor and Barry.

"A box of cookies was taken from the cafeteria during the pizza sale yesterday," Mr. Higgins told the kids.

"Wow!" said Greta. "So that's how they disappeared so quickly."

"How did you find out?" asked Samantha.

"When we counted up our cookie money, we were ten dollars short," explained Barry. "That's exactly how much a box of twenty cookies is worth."

"It was pretty obvious that someone took one," said Mr. Higgins. "This morning, Eleanor finally told us she saw you take it."

"Me?" exclaimed Peter.

"Yeah," said Eleanor. "I saw you running out of the cafeteria door carrying the box."

"But we were sitting on one side of the cafeteria and the cookie table was on the other side," said Mortimer. "How could you see anyone who was running out the door?"

"I could tell it was Peter because of the shark on the back of his T-shirt," Eleanor said.

"I also checked with the lunch monitor and she says you left the cafeteria in a big hurry without asking permission," said Mr. Higgins.

"Yeah, I went to wash some pizza sauce off my shirt," said Peter. "But I didn't take the cookies."

"But Peter, I saw you," said Eleanor.

"You should have told me this immediately, Eleanor," said Mr. Higgins.

"I just didn't want to get Peter in trouble," Eleanor said.

"I don't think that's why you waited," said Greta. "I think you just didn't want to get yourself into trouble."

"What do you mean?" said Eleanor.

"You took the cookies," said Greta.

Why does Greta think Eleanor took the chocolate chip cookies?

"You said it was Peter so you wouldn't be blamed," said Greta.

Eleanor knew she was caught. She confessed that she had stuck the box of cookies in her book bag.

"Sorry about that, Peter," Mr. Higgins said.

"That's okay," said Peter. "I'm just glad my shark and I are off the hook."

46

SOLUTION:
The Case of the Stolen Cookies

"Why do you think that, Greta?" said Mr. Higgins.

"Eleanor said she knew it was Peter running out the lunchroom door because she saw the shark on the back of his T-shirt," said Greta. "But she couldn't have seen that."

"Why not?" asked Mr. Higgins.

"Because there isn't any shark on the back of that T-shirt," Greta answered.

"That's right," said Mortimer. "It's on the *front*. The back is just plain white."

"You took the cookies," said Greta. "You didn't think anyone would notice."

"Yeah!" said Peter. "You didn't know anyone would count up the money."

"But when Barry added it up, everyone knew there was exactly one box missing," said Samantha.

The Case of the Planted Evidence

To celebrate Earth Day in April, the school decided to plant two apple trees. The eighth-grade class was going to do the planting — even digging the holes for the trees. Other classes also had special events planned for later that day. The Clue Jr. Club kids were excited because their fourth-grade class was going to watch a video on Johnny Appleseed after lunch.

Ms. Redding told her class to go straight to the library after lunch instead of coming back to the room. "It's a long video," she explained. "If we meet in the library, we'll save time."

On the morning of Earth Day, all the students gathered on the grass outside the school. The eighth grade began digging two holes — one on each side of the sidewalk leading up to the library door. During the tree planting, Bart Bleach, who was in Ms. Redding's class, and another fourth-grader, Elwood Emerald, started pushing each other. The principal, Mr. Higgins, told them to stop, but a few minutes later the boys were arguing again.

"That's enough, boys," said Mr. Higgins. "I want you both to come in for detention after school. You can use the time to think of better ways to get along."

"But Mr. Higgins," said Bart, "I can't serve detention today. I have an important wrestling match."

"I'm sorry, Bart," said Mr. Higgins. "Next time you feel like fighting, remember to save it for wrestling."

"This isn't fair," said Bart. "This is all Elwood's fault. This wouldn't have happened if he hadn't taken my lucky wrestling charm. Now he's going to make me miss my big match."

"What?" said Elwood. "I don't have your charm, Bart."

"What's this about a lucky wrestling charm, Bart?" asked Mr. Higgins.

"It's a *W* on a chain," answered Bart. "My grandmother gave it to me for good luck. I always carry it with me, and Elwood took it."

"Liar!" yelled Elwood. "I didn't touch your stupid charm."

"Quiet!" said Mr. Higgins. "You boys come with me. You can stay in my office until the tree planting is over."

Mr. Higgins marched the boys off and the eighth-graders finished planting the trees. On the way back to class, Mortimer said, "I'm glad we have the first lunch period. Watching them plant those apple trees made me hungry."

"Then we go watch the video," said Samantha.

"I like these kinds of school days," said Peter. "Very little school."

After lunch, Ms. Redding's class headed to the library. The blinds were drawn and the VCR was ready. Ms. Redding was

right about the video being long. It ended just as the bell rang to change classes. "Perfect timing," laughed Ms. Redding as she turned on the lights. "All right, class. Hurry and line up to go back to the class-room."

As soon as the class got back to their classroom, Bart raised his hand.

"Yes, Bart?" Ms. Redding said.

"I saw Elwood bury something in the dirt under one of the apple trees the eighth-graders planted this morning," he told her.

"When?" she asked.

"Back in the library," Bart said. "He was on the playground during second lunch pe-riod. That's when he has lunch. I saw him out the window digging around the tree when no one was looking. He took some-thing out of his pocket and buried it."

Ms. Redding called Mr. Gleamington, the janitor, on the intercom and asked him to check the soil around the tree. In a few minutes, he came into Ms. Redding's class.

"Is this what you were looking for?" the janitor asked. He handed Ms. Redding a chain. Hanging from it was a charm in the shape of a *W*.

"That's it!" said Bart. "That's my lucky wrestling charm. Elwood grabbed it from me this morning."

Ms. Redding sighed. "I guess we'll have to get Elwood and go to the principal's office," she said. "Mr. Higgins can settle this."

Peter waved his hand in the air. "Wait, Ms. Redding," he said.

"What is it, Peter?" Ms. Redding asked.

"I don't think Elwood buried the charm," Peter answered.

"No?" she said. "Then how did it get under the tree?"

"I think Bart buried it to get Elwood in trouble," said Peter.

Why does Peter think Bart buried his own lucky charm?

my wrestling match today," he said. "I thought maybe Mr. Higgins would let me out of detention if I could make him think Elwood took my charm."

"Instead, you might wind up serving two detentions, not just one," said Ms. Redding.

"Looks like your lucky wrestling charm isn't very lucky for you, Bart," said Peter.

54

SOLUTION:
The Case of the Planted Evidence

"Explain yourself, Peter," said Ms. Redding.

"Bart couldn't have seen Elwood bury anything outside during second lunch period," answered Peter.

"Why not?" asked Ms. Redding.

"Because he couldn't see out of the window," replied Peter.

"That's right," said Mortimer. "We were in the library and the shades were down."

"So the room would be dark for the video," added Greta.

"If Bart had opened a shade to look outside, everyone would have seen the light and seen him do it," said Samantha.

"Well, I think we've seen the light now," said Ms. Redding sternly. "Bart, what do you have to say for yourself?"

Bart admitted that he had tried to get Elwood in trouble. "I don't want to miss

7

The Case of the Sleepover Slumber

On Saturday, the Clue Jr. Club kids were having their weekly Clue Jr. meeting in Mortimer's clubhouse. When Samantha and Greta arrived at ten o'clock, Mortimer's mother told them Mortimer wasn't there. "He'll be back soon," she said. "He spent the night at Peter's and they got up late."

In a few minutes, the boys showed up. Mortimer was wearing one of Peter's T-shirts and a pair of Peter's shorts. "Sorry we're late," said Mortimer. "Mr. Plum let us stay up and watch the late movie and then we overslept."

"That's okay," said Samantha. "I like your new outfit."

Mortimer looked down at the clothes he

was wearing and laughed. "I didn't know I was going to spend the night when I went over to Peter's yesterday, so I didn't take any clean clothes," he said. "He gave me some to wear."

"Well, let's get started," said Greta eagerly. "I've got an idea how we can get to the mall to see that new mystery movie that just opened."

The kids headed for the clubhouse, but the meeting didn't start right away. As soon as everyone was inside, Mortimer began telling them about the new goldfish he had to have, called a comet.

"That's great, Mortimer," Greta said. "But let's talk about the new mystery movie. You can tell us about your fish later."

Just then Harry Henna knocked on the clubhouse door. "Hi, Harry!" Mortimer said. "Come on in." Greta rolled her eyes.

"Hey, Mortimer," Harry said. "I came by to tell you that the pet store just got in a bunch of comets." Harry also collected goldfish. In fact, he and Mortimer often competed to get special fish that came into the pet store.

"Yeah, I know," Mortimer said. "And there are a lot of them. Plenty for both of us."

"Well, I have to go home and clean my room now," Harry said, making a face. "I'll see you at the pet store, Mortimer. Remember, it opens at noon."

"I know," said Mortimer. After Harry left, Mortimer told the kids about a special deal the pet store was offering. "The first two people to buy a comet will win some cool blue coral from New Zealand. You should see it. It's perfect for my tank."

"But isn't the store open already?" Peter asked.

"Nope," Mortimer said. He pointed to a wall calendar hanging in the clubhouse. "Today it opens at noon. I think they're opening late today so they can get ready for a sale they're having. I wrote the time

down on my calendar so I wouldn't forget. We may have to leave our Clue Jr. meeting a little early. Is that okay?"

"Sure," said Samantha. "We can always come back and finish our meeting."

"Finish?" exclaimed Greta. "We haven't even started yet!"

"Oh, wait!" said Mortimer. He turned around and headed back to the house.

"Now what?" sighed Greta. She crossed her arms and slumped down in her seat.

"I need to get my clock from my room so I know what time it is," said Mortimer. "My watch is broken, and I'm not taking any chances on getting to the pet store late."

"But there's no electricity in the club-house," said Greta.

"I have a windup clock," said Mortimer.

Samantha asked, "Why don't you have a clock that uses batteries? That way you don't have to worry about winding it."

"I've had this clock for a while and it works great. I just wind it every night before I go to bed and everything is fine," Mortimer said.

Then Mortimer ran into his house. When he returned, he set the small clock on a shelf where he could see it. "Okay," he said. "It's twenty after ten. We have to leave at eleven-thirty to get to the pet store on time."

Finally Mortimer called the Clue Jr. meeting to order. "At last!" said Greta.

But at ten-thirty, Mortimer interrupted the meeting again. "Listen. Peter and I overslept, so we didn't have any breakfast," he told the others. "Is anybody else hungry?"

"I am!" said Peter. "Let's raid your refrigerator."

"At this rate, we're never going to have our meeting," said Greta.

The kids piled into the house and fixed some frozen waffles. After they cleaned up, they headed back to the clubhouse. It was eleven-fifteen when they returned.

"See," Mortimer said. "We weren't gone long. And we don't have to leave until eleven-thirty."

"Great, a fifteen-minute meeting!" said Greta, shaking her head.

At eleven-thirty, Mortimer grabbed his clock off the shelf and held it up in front of the others. "It's time to head for the pet store," he announced, putting the clock in his pocket.

"Of course," Greta said. "Let's go."

But when they arrived, the store was open and full of people.

"Oh, no!" cried Mortimer. "The store must have opened early!"

When they walked inside, Harry ran over to Mortimer. "Look what I got!" he exclaimed. He held out a piece of blue coral. "There was this deal. I was the first person to buy a comet, so I got this neat coral from New Zealand."

"I thought the store was opening late today," Mortimer said.

"It did," Harry answered. "It opened at noon."

"But we left in plenty of time to get here by noon," said Mortimer. He pulled his clock out of his pocket. It read noon.

"No," said Harry, looking at the clock and then at his watch. "It's twelve-thirty. The store has been open for half an hour."

"My clock is slow!" Mortimer cried. He turned to Harry. "You did this," he shouted. "You came back to the clubhouse while we were inside eating. You set my clock back so you could get the special coral."

"You're nuts, Mortimer," Harry told him. "I came over once to tell you about the comets. I didn't even know about the coral. You probably just forgot to wind your clock."

"No way! I wind my clock every night before I go to bed," said Mortimer.

"Wait a minute! Wait a minute!" said

Peter. "I know why your clock is slow, Mortimer, and it isn't Harry's fault."

"Well, who else would have set it back?" Mortimer asked.

"You did," said Peter. "Sort of."

Why does Peter say Mortimer set his own clock back?

SOLUTION:
The Case of the Sleepover Slumber

"I did?" cried Mortimer. "That's crazy. Why would I do that?"

"You didn't do it on purpose," Peter explained. "You just didn't wind it."

"But I always wind it every night before I go to bed," said Mortimer.

"Right," said Peter. "And where was your clock last night?"

"In my room by my bed, where it always is," said Mortimer.

"And where were you last night?" Peter asked.

"I was . . ." Mortimer began. Then he shut his mouth. "Oh."

"You weren't in your room last night!" cried Greta. "You were at Peter's house."

"You didn't wind your clock last night," said Peter, "so it slowed down a half hour."

"I guess you're right," said Mortimer. "I'm really sorry, Harry."

"That's okay, Mortimer," said Harry. "If you hurry and buy your comet now, I bet you can still get some coral."

"Great!" exclaimed Mortimer. He found a salesclerk and got his fish and his coral. "I was in time after all," he told everyone.

"Now maybe we have time for the rest of our Clue Jr. meeting," laughed Greta.

66

8

The Case of the Soccer Camp Mystery

Greta was away at sleepaway soccer camp and the Greens had invited the Clue Jr. Club kids to go with them on visitors' day. "Tell your parents we won't be home until late," they told the kids. "There's a soccer game after dinner, and we won't be leaving until after that."

In the car on the way to the camp, Mrs. Green held up a soccer shirt to show the kids. On the front was a picture of a woman kicking a soccer ball with the name *Tina LaCosta* written underneath. The number *42* was on the back of the shirt.

"Who's Tina LaCosta?" asked Mortimer.

"She's Greta's favorite player," said Mrs. Green. "She's from South America, where soccer is more popular than in the United States. You wouldn't believe how hard it was to find this shirt, because this woman isn't very well known here. But Greta loves soccer so much and works so hard at it that we thought we'd reward her with something she'll really like."

At the camp all the visitors got a tour of the grounds. The soccer field even had lights so the kids could play at night. On one side of the field were the boys' cabins and on the other side were the girls' cabins. There was also a lake where the campers and their visitors went swimming that afternoon. Later, everyone had dinner in the camp mess hall. Greta showed the other campers her Tina LaCosta shirt at dinner.

"Wow!" said Roberta Ruddy. "I can't believe you have a shirt with Tina LaCosta on it."

"I know!" said her sister, Randi. "Can I borrow it?" She took the shirt and held it against her. "Fits perfectly!"

"Sorry," said Greta, taking her shirt from Randi, "but this is an extra-special shirt — Tina LaCosta is my favorite player."

After dinner, the head counselor announced that the boys' teams would play at six-thirty, then the girls' teams would play at eight o'clock. "You should walk around and relax for a while," she told the campers. "Let your dinner settle so you'll be ready to play."

"There's no way I can play tonight, no matter how long I relax," said Randi. Randi was on Greta's team, but she had twisted her ankle during practice that afternoon.

"It stinks that Randi can't play tonight," Greta told the Clue Jr. kids. "She's one of the best players on our team. I really want to win tonight. The winning team gets an award and a celebration in the mess hall after the game."

"Don't worry, Greta," Randi said. "You don't need me to win. I'll be watching the game from my cabin's porch."

The Clue Jr. kids walked around the lake until it was time for the boys to play. After the first game, they walked with Greta to join her teammates. Suddenly Mortimer stopped and looked up. "Hey! Check out the moon," he said. He pointed to a huge full moon high in the evening sky.

"It's so bright that you could probably play without the lights, Greta," said Samantha.

"Good luck," called Peter to Greta as the three friends took a seat on the bleachers.

"I know you'll win," said Mortimer.

Greta's team did win. She scored once and blocked three shots that were going straight for her team's goal. After the game, everyone headed for the mess hall to eat cake and ice cream and cheer the winning teams.

"Wait! I want to wear my new Tina La-Costa shirt to the mess hall," said Greta. "Come back to my cabin with me to get it, guys." When the Clue Jr. Club kids reached the cabin, Greta stopped at the front door. "There's Randi," she said, pointing to the cabin next to hers. "She's sitting on her porch with Roberta. Let's see how she's feeling."

Just then Randi called out, "Hey, Greta! Good job. You blocked three shots and even scored!"

"Thanks. How's your ankle?" Greta asked.

"Better," said Randi. "Roberta didn't play, either. She felt sick to her stomach and had to sit on the sideline."

"Too bad!" said Greta. "I didn't know that. I didn't see you on the side."

"No wonder," said Roberta with a smile. "You were a one-girl team."

"Can you come to the mess hall and have dessert with everyone?" Greta asked them.

"I guess so," said Randi. "I can walk better now."

"Yeah," said Roberta. "I want to support the team."

"Great," said Greta. "Wait just a minute.

I'm going to get my Tina LaCosta shirt." She ran up to her cabin with the Clue Jr. kids. The box containing Greta's new shirt lay on her bunk, but when she opened the box, there was no shirt inside.

"My shirt is gone!" she cried.

"Someone must have taken it during the soccer game," said Peter.

"That could be anyone," said Mortimer. "You showed it to the whole camp."

"Wait! Randi was sitting on the porch next door during the game," said Samantha. "Let's see if she saw anyone go into the cabin."

When the kids asked her, Randi said she saw a couple of people enter the cabin. "Who?" said Greta excitedly.

"Sorry, Greta. It was too dark to see their faces," said Randi.

"Oh," said Greta, disappointed.

"Let's tell the counselors at the mess hall," said Randi. "They can keep a lookout for it."

"Okay," said Greta sadly.

On the way to the mess hall, Peter pulled on Greta's arm. "I didn't see Roberta sitting on the sideline," he whispered. "Maybe she faked being sick so she could sneak into your cabin and get your shirt."

Greta shrugged. "Maybe. But how can we find out for sure?"

At the mess hall, Greta told the counselors about her stolen shirt.

"Well, there's still a week of camp left," said one counselor. "Maybe we can find it. After all, there's only one like it."

"Maybe we don't have to wait to catch the thief," said Mortimer.

"Do you have a clue, Mortimer?" asked Greta.

"I think I do," he answered. "A big round one."

"What?" said Peter.

"The moon," said Mortimer. "And the moon tells me Randi took the shirt."

Why does Mortimer think Randi took Greta's shirt?

SOLUTION:
The Case of the Soccer Camp Mystery

"That's not very nice, Mortimer," said Randi angrily. "Besides, it's stupid! How can the moon tell you I took Greta's shirt?"

"What do you mean, Mortimer?" asked the counselor.

"Randi, you were sitting on the porch of your cabin for the whole game, right?" said Mortimer.

"Right," she answered.

"And you saw some kids go into Greta's cabin, but it was too dark to see who they were," said Mortimer. Randi nodded.

"But you recognized Greta when she was walking up to the cabin," said Mortimer. "It wasn't too dark then."

"I get it!" exclaimed Peter. "The moon! The full moon was so bright that Randi could recognize Greta."

"If you recognized Greta, you could

have recognized the other kids, too," said Samantha. "Which means you're lying."

"And why would you lie unless you took the shirt yourself?" said Mortimer.

Randi confessed that she took the shirt and would give it back.

"So that's what you meant when you said the moon told you it was Randi, Mortimer," giggled Samantha.

"Yeah. I guess the moon shed some light on this mystery," laughed Mortimer.